PRAISE FOR THE AUTHOR

"Starting with poignant explorations of grief and the difficult, dangerous tangle of love and frustration between siblings, tensions in Emily Ruth Verona's Shiva quickly ratchet to a white-knuckle, breath-stealing finish. I could not put this one down. A sharp and stunningly beautiful ghost story."

—Jaima Fixsen, USA Today-bestselling author of Specimen

"Shiva is a startling exploration of grief, guilt, and spite through reverie, body horror, and unreliable narrators, unpacking a complex sibling relationship centered around what has been left unfinished."

—Ai Jiang, Bram Stoker Award-winning author of Linghun

"Verona is unflinching in her portrayal of a sibling bond battered and stretched to its limits by guilt, frustration, resentment, and all the ugliness that comes with love. Shiva is grief horror as vicious and heartbreaking as family itself."

—J. A. W. McCarthy, Bram Stoker and Shirley Jackson Award finalist, author of Sleep Alone

"Intricately nuanced and unflinching, *Shiva* is a compulsive read that portrays grief with startling honesty. Verona's storytelling cuts deep in her latest work, where compassion is brandished as the knife hidden behind your back."

Grace R. Reynolds, Elgin Award-nominated author of
The Lies We Weave and *Neon Moon*

"Verona knocks it out of the park… The beginning of what's sure to be an incredible career."

—Gwendolyn Kiste, four-time Bram Stoker Award-wining author of *The Haunting of Velkwood* and *Reluctant Immortals*

"A dazzling new voice in suspense."

—Wendy Webb, bestselling author of
Daughters of the Lake

"Horror fans will delight."

—*Publishers Weekly*

SHIVA

Other Books by Emily Ruth Verona
Midnight on Beacon Street (2024, Harper Perennial)

Copyright © 2026 Emily Ruth Verona

This book is a work of fiction. Any reference to historical events, real people, or real places are used fictitiously. Other names, characters, places, and events are products of the author's or artist's imagination, and any resemblance to actual events or places or persons, living or dead, is entirely coincidental.

All rights reserved. No part of this book may be reproduced or used in any manner without the prior written permission of the copyright owner, except for the use of brief quotations in a book review.

Edited by Maddy Leary
Book Design and Layout by Rob Carroll
Cover Design by Rob Carroll

Library of Congress Control Number: 2026933594

ISBN 978-1-958598-93-1 (paperback)
ISBN 979-8-9933676-0-6 (eBook)

darkmatter-ink.com

SHIVA

EMILY RUTH VERONA

For you, Mom—
Love you lots and acres

DAY ONE

EVA

I AM THE object of pity here. The fragile. The bereaved. So delicate they expect me to fall to pieces. Only, my pieces look better when taken apart. Laid out like shards of colored glass for some avant-garde mosaic. The less sense I make, the more like myself I feel. After all, loose fragments can be used to make great art—tastefully contorted in a mock-up of beauty. Nothing about me has ever been tasteful though. Or beautiful. Even the hurt feels too dull to satisfy.

In that regard, I guess I was already prepared to lose him—had lost him, over and over again through the years. The bonds of family stretch like a worn-out sweater. Shape. Style. Feel. Until that sweater is unrecognizable in its shabbiness. This is what we'd become to one another. Cheap sweaters destined for the rag bin. Not worth a yard sale or a donation basket.

Twice now I've smile-frowned at the same set of cousins I can't quite name. That's such a funeral-ish thing, isn't it? Smiling and frowning at the same time. As if to say *good for you, you're getting through it*, but in a way that does not convey enthusiasm unbefitting the occasion. If they circle back around the room again for another peek at my black eye, I swear to God I'm going to give them a hearty thumbs-up. Just puff my cheeks out and expand my grotesqueness like a goddamn puffer fish. They're here to gawk. It's the only reason they're here—the reason most people are here. To get a glimpse of the wreck—the Drucker who made it out alive. *Wahoo!* Cheaper than a movie. Less tactless than standing by the side of the road staring at a totaled car, shoving mouthfuls of popcorn in your face—not that there's much difference, save for the ceremony. No flashing lights here. No sirens. Only the quiet dignity of dissolution. The Mourner's Kaddish as we say goodbye.

I thought the rabbi might act as a buffer of some kind, but he is *nowhere* in sight. This thing is going to start soon…there must be some joke about an absentee rabbi, right? One could probably affix *rabbi* or *priest* or any religious figurehead to the punchline and draw a laugh. The absoluteness of such positions, perhaps. The big, looming certainty of their faith. It's bound to make anyone skittish. And when people get skittish, they do strange things. They pick at their cuticles. They smile at funerals. Their inner monologue starts to rhyme.

There's a eulogy coming up that I can't give. Won't give. Nope. No way. Not me. Because doing that will seal this day as one which has come to pass and then…what, exactly? Tomorrow will tag in followed by the day after that, and the day after that, and the day after that. Seven days of sitting shiva and then *bam*! All done. *Congratulations. You've buried the dead. On to the next stage of your life!*

But it's impossible. What I'm expected to do here is impossible. Because I loved him, when all is said and done and catalogued for posterity. He was my brother and he was all I had—even when I didn't have him at all—and now I won't ever have him again. It shouldn't surprise me. It shouldn't it shouldn't it shouldn't. But we were always going to end like this. My dumbass brother was always going to die. And I was always going to let him.

THOMAS

THE SLEEVES ARE too long. Rolling them up would look even weirder, right? Best to leave them—even if cuffs down to my palms make me look like a little boy. *Fuck*. No wonder I haven't made it inside. Lurking by the back entrance…anyone might mistake me for a waiter trying to bum a smoke. Except for this goddamn jacket. Practically a wedding tux.

Evie had it at her apartment, which shouldn't surprise me. It's her dad's from…his second marriage? Third? Who knows. She kept anything and everything. Pack rat style. I don't know how she got a hold of this suit. Hell, it's probably something she pulled out of his house after he died. A dead man's suit. That's something, huh? I told her back when she was selling his house that she should get rid of his shit, but when did Evie ever listen to anything I told her? She said I couldn't appreciate her perspective on it, that she didn't want to look back one day and regret having sold or pawned or given away his junk just because she'd spent so many years being mad at him.

SHIVA

Well, I guess she was right—not that she would have figured how right. I needed something to wear to this damn thing and good ole Evie came through. A problem solver, my sister. Through and through. Someone bent on fixing things that shouldn't be fixed. And if she met someone she couldn't fix? Hell...Evie wouldn't know what to do with the poor son of a bitch. Which is probably why she cut me out of her life—what, five? Ten? A dozen times?

You know, that girl threw herself out a window the day I was born. What would they say if I went in and told that story, huh? It's a fun one if you ignore the beginning, the middle, and the end. According to Mom, Evie was home with a babysitter, and after word reached the house that the family now had a healthy baby boy joining the ranks, my four-year-old big sister went and jumped out a window.

It was a first-floor window, but a window all the same. Wide open because of the summer heat, with a screen that could never quite stay in. She stepped off that sill and fell right into a bush. They were picking nettles out of her hair for weeks after. That's the Evie I know. Excessive. Manipulative. She probably orchestrated all of this as a punishment. The ultimate long con. *Here, little brother. You want this family? I've been looking for an out since the day you were born and now, I'm gone for good.*

Maybe they won't notice if I don't go inside. The temptation to leave, it's strong as hell, but—something inside of me is worried that if I'm not here for her now then no one else will be. Might not be worry. Might just be indigestion. But, still. Her dad is dead. Our mom deader. None of these so-called relatives here could have picked her out of a lineup. So, who does she have left? Me, apparently. *Fuck.*

I shove a sleeve up, but it slips back down again. Extending my shoulder, I try to stretch my wrist—elongate my arm. It doesn't work. *Double fuck.*

How about this: What if I go inside but hang in the hallway, does that count? It wouldn't be bailing—not really. It would be…something else. I don't know what. But it wouldn't count as leaving. It would just be…not following through. That couldn't surprise anyone, least of all Evie. Yeah. I can just hang in the back. Keep a low profile, then come outside and wait for the snow to fall. It's supposed to snow today. They said so on the radio. I'm not giving a eulogy or anything—that old woman she used to work with is doing it. Thank God. I wouldn't be able to string two words together—let alone however many it takes to put someone in the ground. I'd end up telling the jumping-out-the-window story. Make a real mess of things. Because I can't do this. I need a way out. An excuse. I'd walk into the street and wait for a bike to hit me if I thought it would do any good.

Of course, maiming me and some cyclist won't fix the fact that this thing is going to happen whether I want it to or not. This service is moving forward. Doesn't matter where I go or what I do. Except that it probably does matter. It wouldn't be so hard if it didn't.

The sky is all dark and gray and ominous now—and only getting darker, too.

Appropriate, given everything. Real funeral weather. Because the truth is that Evie is dead. She's dead and there's no way to slice it that doesn't make it my fault.

DAY TWO

EVA

THE THINGS WE remember. We don't choose them, not always, not most of the time. One of my earliest memories is Thomas hitting me in the face with a xylophone mallet. He was two. I was six. Our grandmother had given us this little toy xylophone for Chanukah, but she just gave us the one. We fought over it constantly. I don't remember the pain or my nose bleeding, even though blood got all over the carpet. My clothes. The xylophone. Instead, I remember the swing.

The little red ball at the end of the wooden stick cutting through the air. The shock on Thomas's small face, because even before the blow had struck, he'd regretted what he'd done. Regretted—but went through with it anyway. Recognizing the harm it would do. Knowing that the result would hurt me. That's my brother in a nutshell for you. He was the kind of person who would apologize before, not after, hitting you in the face. As if apology and regret are interchangeable.

Memory is a fucked-up thing. It's bizarre that we can relive a single moment over and over through the years without any recollection of what directly preceded or followed it. No beginning. No end. Just the middle. And from that middle, and perhaps a dozen more middles like it, we're shaped into who we are. Yeah. Memory is definitely a fucked-up thing. But aren't we all fucked up, too?

This is the latest in a long line of grotesquely self-indulgent notions to coil around my brain as Francine shifts her hands, placing one over the other and then back again. She does this whenever I've been sitting silent for too long. A subtle reminder to come back to her. I smile, knowing just how fraudulent that U-shaped line looks on my face. "Don't give me that," I say, irritable. I've been quiet and moody since the funeral, but really—longer than that. My whole life, likely. *You always look like someone just stole your lunch money.* That's what my brother used to say.

"Give you what, dear?"

I want to groan. "*Those eyes.*"

Francine sits back in her chair, shoulders squaring. She's sharper at seventy-five than I ever have been or ever will be, but I don't tell her that. Because she would scoff and wave it off and insist that if I can't be honest, I shouldn't say anything at all. It's the truth though. I swear it. Thomas always says—always said—that my truths sound more like lies. Maybe he was right. The thought makes my stomach roll. It's like being on a roller coaster that has just flipped upside-down—or something less stereotypical than but just as visceral as some dumb roller coaster. "You're giving me those eyes, which means you're wondering what I had for breakfast," I tell her. "You want to know if how worried you are is in sync with how worried you should be."

A pause. "And is it?"

"Honestly? I have no fucking idea."

Swearing is a habit I picked up from Francine a long time ago and it makes her smirk. Before college I was all

SHIVA

*darn*s and *frigging*s. "I'm not worried. *Worry* and *sympathy* and *sorry*…all valid sentiments but none of them mean what anyone is ever trying to say in using them."

I offer an audible sound of agreement. Not that it satisfies. Shiva should be sat at home. That's technically the tradition. It's what we did for my dad. Mom, too. But the thought of people crammed into my apartment with casseroles and long faces. I'd rather pull my own damn fingernails off and eat them.

"What I feel for you is love," Francine continues. "And a frustration that I cannot take away the emotions that you have to experience right now."

With a sad smile I reach out and take one of her hands in my own, kiss the smooth, soft skin above her knuckles. She is good to me. A better mentor than I have ever deserved. Almost like a second mother. One who could actually be patient with me. "I know. Thank you."

Francine adjusts her posture. She has the posture of a ballerina, unusual for a professor, and has always reminded me of the English actress Charlotte Rampling. Elegant. Confident. Poised. With eyes that can cut steel. "Have you dreamt yet?" Francine asks. It's meant to catch me off guard and it does.

Some people talk about having nightmares after experiencing trauma, but I haven't been able to recall a single dream—nightmare or otherwise—since my brother died. I can't tell if that's more or less concerning than seeing him every time I close my eyes. His face should be an intrusive thorn in my brain, but I haven't experienced anything like that. Usually, obsessive-compulsive disorder makes it impossible not to picture unwanted images in my head. This…this is the opposite. Maybe there's an inversion of OCD called apathetic-denial disorder. Only, that wouldn't work. The acronym is already taken.

Not dreaming wouldn't be so weird if not for the fact that I have always been an elaborate dreamer. My cinematic subconscious is prone to sparing no details in the construction of dramatic illusions. My brain has always worked that way—acutely visual. That's why my OCD symptoms have always been rooted in seeing. Observing. It's also why Francine chose me to be the TA for her World Art course way back when even though I'd only been a sophomore at the time. I was thorough. More than thorough. Nothing ever slipped by me. The O in OCD doesn't just come from nowhere.

But after the accident…

The doctors and Francine attribute this to the concussion, but I think it's more than that. I wouldn't mind so much if it cured the OCD along with it, but obsessive-compulsive isn't the kind of thing you cure. It's how you're wired. How I'm wired. And I'm still experiencing all my usual compulsions. Just the dreams won't come.

Francine and I sit in silence, me holding her hand and her letting me. I don't answer her question and I don't know how much time passes, but the simpleness of not having to say anything right away is nice and so we both let it stretch—silence smoothing out in front of us like a linen tablecloth at a fancy restaurant. It almost feels good. Meaningful. But it can't last. Nothing does.

"What comes next?" I ask when silence is no longer sustainable. I've done this before. I should know how it goes. But with Thomas it feels different. "After the grieving, then what?"

Francine leans back in her chair. "You're not done with the grieving yet, dear."

"But when I am?"

"Focus on the now. What can you do now—with where you are and what you are feeling."

SHIVA

I shrug. Not for her, just for me. So I can feel like the irresponsible, insolent teenager my brother always thought I was, but in reality, never got to be.

"Eva…"

"I could get hammered." The wistful way in which I mention this comes across as far more dreamy—far more eager—than I intended. Her lips tighten in response, outlining the wrongness of it.

Francine doesn't fault me, though. Her eyes remain kind. Clear. Full of empathy. "And then?" she asks. I don't have an answer to that either, which is of course her point. My mouth shrivels into a sour line.

"It's what he would do," I say. "If Thomas were the one here right now—he'd go to The Martyred Mare. He'd go to The Martyred Mare and get drunk out of his head and he wouldn't apologize to anyone—least of all me—for doing it."

THOMAS

I'M NOT DRUNK. That's something, at least. I've needed a whiskey all fucking day but when I finally walked down to bar tonight, all I ordered was a Coke. I've been sipping steadily on that for half an hour now. I don't understand why I won't let myself get the whiskey. Evie, probably. Somehow, in death my sister's opinion suddenly holds more weight than it ever did when she was alive. She'd hate it if I got shit-faced because she's dead, but not because she'd feel bad for me or anything like that. She'd hate it because it would mean I'm taking attention away from her, away from the loss of her somehow, and putting it on myself. Selfish. If I got shit-faced right now, she'd call it selfish. Even if it would be selfish of her to say so.

Twice now I've called the bartender over only to wave him off again. I better tip well on this soda or he'll piss in the next one. It's Friday night and the place is packed. Bodies pressed together in that way where the smell of sweat and beer blend into one another. I shouldn't be taking up space at the counter with my buck fifty tab. But I don't know where else to go. And I still want that

SHIVA

whiskey. My fingers *tap tap tap* against the counter like the chattering of teeth. It's hard to sit still.

But I'm not drunk. Not yet. And that's something. Right?

A girl crowds in close to me to order a drink. Short, bobbed hair and frizzy bangs. She looks just like Evie, which is why I stare longer than I should. When this girl notices, a frown carves out the bottom of her mouth and she leans away, towards the hipsters standing on the other side. *Fuck.* I'm that guy now. The creepy loner too drunk to see straight, only I'm not drunk and I can see straight so that just leaves creepy. Excellent. Bravo. Well done. Evie always said I'd get there eventually. Mess is only tempting when you're young. What a girl might find mysterious at fifteen is sad at twenty-five. Ugly at thirty-five. I don't know how much of it is showing now but it's enough that the girl with the bangs can see the effect of it spread all around my body like a series of terminal tumors—you know, the kind that grow on the backs of rats. Who the hell wants to be around something like that? No one. Absolutely fucking no one. I would cut myself out of me if I could.

Once she has a drink in her hand, the girl with the bob makes an eager retreat. Her place at the counter is quickly seized by a taller woman with a long, slender neck and piercing flame-blue eyes. The confidence with which she shifts her weight in heels and ignores me is a turn-on. A lot to unpack there, as Evie and her six years of therapy would say. *Why do you want women who don't see you? Why are you so desperate for them to validate your existence?* Surely, she'd attribute it to childhood. Me having something to prove. We were always so different in that respect. I was the one who wanted to stand out—get someone, anyone, to notice him. But not her. Even with her dramatic flair. Attention would bore into her soul like the almighty wrath of God. She'd do just about anything to ensure that no one saw her. No one spoke to her. No one disturbed the casing she had so carefully constructed around herself. She'd never admit she wanted that attention, either. No matter how true it was.

I had a friend once who said there was too much hate in my sister. I insisted that she wasn't the hateful kind, but he said not outwardly hateful. Inwardly hateful. He said that sometimes we hate ourselves because we think we can get away with it. That no one will stop us—or maybe because we want to see if someone will stop us. And when they don't, well, we go ahead and hate ourselves all the more for it. He was probably right. but he was wasted at the time, we both were, so who the fuck knows. Evie never wanted anyone to stop her from being the way she was—would have lashed out like an animal if anyone so much as tried to change her. Not that it ever stopped her from trying to change the rest of us.

The blue-eyed woman sips what looks like a gin and tonic. It's got me actively horny now. *Fuck-itty fuck*. I go to raise my hand for the bartender, but stop myself, slamming a palm down on my half-lifted fingers. I mean, what is there left if not whiskey, huh? How do I control the spiral if there isn't anything to control it with—because, let's be honest, that's what I'm doing here. I'm about to spiral. It's inevitable. My entire goddamn body is catapulting towards it. But I need fuel. I need something destructive, but manageable. Because tomorrow I still have to wake up and be here. A hangover, that is manageable. A punch to the gut rather than permanent tearing inside the abdomen. Just enough wrong to feel right. I can work with that.

Again, I hold up a hand. This time, I don't change my mind. I call the bartender over, order a whiskey, and throw it back in one swig before ordering another.

EVA

THERE ARE FIFTEEN cracks in the ceiling paint. I've counted them again and again. Four long ones, like loose spider legs. Two deep ones, because the paint was applied too thick in those areas and has since cracked, and nine small ones, like little hairline fractures. *Four, two, nine.* Even in the dark I can see them, read them like a constellation in the sky. One that might guide me home. Only, I am home. And I'm lonely. So goddamn lonely.

I roll over, abandoning all pretense of sleep, and grab my phone off the nightstand. A terrible habit. Francine is always saying it's why I'm perpetually tired, looking at that screen every fifteen minutes all night long. I'm sure she's right. But it never stops me. An hour passes, maybe two, as I scroll through true crime blogs and top ten unsolved mystery guides—anything to remind me that being bored and lonesome is nothing compared to the true horrors of the world. This knowledge centers me, eases me into the acceptance of the fact that I won't be sleeping tonight.

At least *15 Unsolved Mysteries You've Never Heard Before* and *8 People Who Escaped Serial Killers* provide listified distractions from what's really bothering me: I can't remember the last thing I said to him. I've been trying all day to figure it out, but that's led nowhere. I didn't know at the time that it would be the last thing and so I hadn't been paying attention. He was talking about something—some record he'd heard, because my brother was an insufferable hipster who only ever listened to records on the secondhand player he'd gotten at the thrift store his ex-girlfriend used to work at—does work at. I don't know. She might still be there. Thomas wasn't exactly the keep-in-touch kind.

Should I have invited her to the service? The ex-girlfriend. Fuck. What if she doesn't even know that he's— no. Impossible. Someone would have said something to her. In this day and age—people don't die quiet anymore. She would have read about it or gotten a text about it or heard from one of his friends. There's no way it could have evaded her attention. And yet—it might have evaded mine, had I not been there. Would they have notified me? I'm not listed as his next of kin. Hell, with different dads, we didn't even have the same last name. No one would have known who to call or what to do if I hadn't been…

Two o'clock in the morning rolls around. I get up and turn the lights on, head to the breakfast table where I never eat breakfast. My latest puzzle is splayed only a third finished atop the plastic surface. Two baby deer standing alone in a wood as snow begins to drift across the foliage. There's a certain level of impossibility to snowy scenes that I find appealing, matching each subtle shift of shade and turn of groove to put the pieces together. Jigsaws help to keep me focused—or rather, they keep me distracted enough that I don't fixate on the wrong things. How tired I am. How much I want tequila even though I'm not supposed to be drinking on my meds. How my

SHIVA

brother always thought these puzzles were a waste of time. He didn't see the point in putting something together only to break it apart again. Maybe if I glued the pieces in and displayed them, he would have let it go, but I don't. When a puzzle is done, I take a picture for my own vain posterity and pack all the pieces up again and donate the gently used box to a local after school program. It's not the having, it's the doing. That's what I tried to explain to him. The satisfaction doesn't come from hoarding accomplishments. I just like the way my body feels when one little piece of cardboard slides in perfectly against another. That small dopamine hit which follows the completion of a particularly challenging area. Similar to unlocking a very good secret. I've always had a thing for secrets. Even Thomas knew that.

THOMAS

"YOUR PLACE IS nice," the blonde croons into my neck as I kick the door closed with my foot. We stumble a little in the dark because I don't know where to find the light switch. She draws away, giggling as she pulls her blouse up over her head and tosses it on the floor. Her bra is a crisscross pattern of straps and sexiness. She turns her head in search of the bedroom, but I pick her up by the hips, twirl her drunkenly as we stumble towards the couch.

She smells like gin and perfume and I breathe her hair in by the fistful while she unbuttons my pants. The room is spinning a little, but in that good way…making everything feel light. Impermanent. Fleeting. A single-dose experience. The only kind that never disappoints.

We're kissing and my hands are all over her and I'm trying to unhook her bra when I see it in a flash. In a wisp. Evie at the table.

It's so jarring I nearly knock the woman atop me onto the floor as the smell of wet earth floods my senses. The blonde grabs my shoulders to brace herself, and I flash her a split, apologetic look before turning back to get a better view of the kitchen table. Only, there's nothing. No ghosts in sight. That weird, musky scent is gone.

Of course. Even if this is my dead sister's apartment. Which is now where I plan to get laid. Because there's nowhere else to go and I had this key on me anyway from…from when I was supposed to be here going through her things instead of picking up this blue-eyed angel with soft, salty skin that almost makes me believe in a goddamn god.

The blonde cups my face in her palms, her finely arched brow pinched in consternation as she tries to determine if I'm too drunk to get it up. Maybe I am. But it won't stop me from trying. So, I plant a series of kisses up and down her neck. And that seems to get us back on track. I tell her she is beautiful and she giggles again, an airy cotton candy sound. By the time her hands are down my pants I don't remember what it was I thought I'd seen at the kitchen table.

I don't remember anything.

And that's just the way I want it.

DAY THREE

EVA

THE LINE AT the coffee shop snakes around the cramped entryway. It's so suffocating and sweaty in here that I almost want to get an iced mocha, even though it's about twenty-five degrees outside. Slowly, with painstaking sluggishness, some space opens up and I manage to inch forward. Those people who are always late to everything—work, social gatherings, appointments—because they stopped to get coffee bother the hell out of me and yet here I am, preparing to join their ranks as a total dick.

I glance down at the broad, round face of my wristwatch. My brother hates—hated—this thing. Said it's too chunky and clunky and old-fashioned. It belonged to our grandfather originally, not that Thomas ever took that into account as to why I might want to wear it. My memories of our grandfather are brief but distinct—more so than Thomas's probably were. He was only four when our grandfather died, but I was eight and missed him enough to relive moments with him in my head throughout the years—over and over—so I wouldn't forget. The way he'd pull me up onto his knee whenever he had a present for me. How he always smelled like fresh bread or cinnamon sugar because he'd owned a bakery for forty-five years and even after he retired, he liked to get up early and spend time in the kitchen. The sugar cookies our mother used to make when we were little—the ones my brother loved—those were his recipe. Sometimes by concentrating, I can even recall the sound of his voice—old and worn, but soothing. Always soothing. Like a cup of hot chocolate on a snowy day.

Will I remember Thomas's voice ten, twenty years from now? Will I put in the effort to make sure I do? The answer should feel immediate—obvious—but it doesn't. My brother had a nice voice, a gentle voice, but it was never kind. It was the type of voice that you want to trust—need to trust—and then the second you do, you regret it. Just like the day he died. I hadn't wanted to go. I hadn't wanted and I hadn't wanted and I hadn't wanted, but he insisted. He insisted and I gave in and now look where we're at.

The short, dark-haired man at the counter pays and steps aside, giving the barista an opportunity to smile a sad funeral smile at me as I step up to place my order. I almost burst out laughing, but I don't. "Hiya there," she chirps. "What can I do for you today?"

Almost immediately I forget what it was I wanted and ask for a small black coffee. After I've paid and the steaming hot cup has been handed to me, I fill it with six packets of sugar and walk outside, palms wrapped around the seething warmth of the paper cup that permeates through the cardboard coffee sleeve. I look down. This isn't my order. It's Thomas's. Strong coffee. Six sugars. He always had to overdo everything. Go big or go home. Fuck it up or fuck off. I can't drink this sugary slop.

I toss it into a garbage bin. Go back in and wait in line all over again.

THOMAS

YEAH. YEAH. I'M slutty when I'm sad. I know this. It's not a big deal. There are worse things to be. And yet as sunlight streams through the blinds, I forget for maybe half a second about the woman curled at the other end of the couch, her feet hooked in mine as she snores softy, her face smooshed against the only pillow. That explains why my neck hurts. I slept against a slanted couch arm and now my head feels equally slanted. I consider standing, but don't. At least I remember last night. Sort of.

Disdain coils around my body. Territorial. Possessive. I am a piece of shit. Bringing someone back here. It's like having sex in your parents' bed or something. I want to scrape last night off, undo every decision I made. Except the sex, of course. That part was all right. Better than all right. At least on her part. I probably could have done better.

There isn't really any way to stand up without waking the blonde and so I stay put, watching the light shift and fade as clouds pass by overhead. I think it's supposed to snow flurry today. Or maybe that was yesterday. Sometimes I wonder if my brain only ever retains information when I'm drinking, that anything I hear or learn while sober just evaporates upon contact.

I used to say the worst god-awful shit to Evie when I was drunk. Back in high school, when I was pilfering my dad's whiskey—the cheap stuff he only resorted to when he was hammered, so he wouldn't know the difference—I used to call Evie up from all kinds of places. Beg her to drive me home. It was never house parties—I was too much of a loser for that. It was usually parks. Shopping centers. Places I'd walk to but then get tired or lost and not have it in me to go all the way back home by myself. Then, when Evie would come and get me—and she always came and got me—I'd find something to shit on. She took too long or her car smelled like that weird gum she liked or she was just acting extra bitchy for no reason. Except the reason was that her fourteen-year-old brother was dragging her out of bed the night before a big History test to come collect his ass. Evie probably thought I was blackout drunk those nights, but I wasn't. I remember every stupid, dumb, ugly thing I ever said to her. Worse still, I even blamed her for them. She always expected me to be a shit brother so I acted like a shit brother. It was her fault, not mine. That's what I told myself.

I'm thirsty, but I can't see a clock. Maybe Evie didn't have one here, except that doesn't sound right. She was always the punctual type. The orderly type. The kind who sent out holiday cards to everyone she'd ever known because she bothered to keep track of them all. She used to even send them to her exes, which I thought was weird as hell. But she always managed to remain friendly—if not exactly friends—with her ex-boyfriends, no matter how rough the breakup. If you ask me, it's because she never really cared about any of them. No. That would have been too scary for Evie. She couldn't risk them letting her down like our mom. Her dad. Me.

The room is bright and almost cheery with sunlight by the time the blonde finally stirs. She rolls over, half awake, and only seems to realize she's on a couch when she reaches out to slap an alarm that isn't there. One eye flutters open, put off by the seemingly sudden presence of daylight. Her head turns and that's when she notices me, her body going rigid. My name is pursed between the curve of her lips and yet she doesn't say it. Because the blonde doesn't know it. And I don't know her name either. She smiles bashfully. "Come here often?" she asks.

An image of Evie at the breakfast table pulses in my brain. "No. Never."

DAY FOUR

EVA

"HOW ARE YOU faring?"

The question feels like needles plunged deep, deep, deep into my skin. Sadistic acupuncture. It's the eighth time someone has asked it today and I'm ready to scream until the world cracks open. But I don't. Because I'm not the screaming kind. And so, I shrug and mumble something innocuous and check the time. It's only ten o'clock. The thought of doing this for seven more hours is enough to make my insides blister. I shouldn't have come back to work today. Everyone looked surprised when I walked through the door this morning, like they'd expected me to take more time. I should have taken more time. It's what a rational person would do. Only, if I spent one more minute counting ceiling cracks, I was going to lose my mind. I need a distraction. Something concrete. Four-dimensional. Engagement with a world that exists outside of my own brain.

The nice thing about sitting at a desk is that there are a thousand ways to busy yourself. I spend the better part of the morning rearranging things, organizing and catching up on the e-mails that stacked up in my inbox during my absence. I choose every word in my responses with excessive care. Lots of *it feels good to be back in the office* and *I hope this e-mail finds you well, let's talk about what we'll say in the brochure over lunch next week*. I like the low-key monotony that comes with responding to e-mails, answering questions and confirming meeting info. It feels vaguely pointless and there is a deeply rooted sense of reassurance in that. Action, reaction. It's orderly, but not overwhelming. Productive but not pungent. Exactly what I need right now.

By noon I'm mostly caught up. Apparently, my assistant and deputy communications manager were able to keep things afloat in my absence, proving that all marketing firms are oversaturated and could probably function with half the time, staff, and effort expected from a business of this stature. I consider quitting. Not intentionally. It just enters my head, like a bubble about to pop, and once it does the notion vanishes just as quickly. It happens at least six times a week. Not that I've ever acted on it. I need my monotony. It's what keeps me safe.

That day with my brother, that day was unexpected. Out of the ordinary. And look what happened. Remembering it makes my stomach twist like it's eating itself from the inside out. Maybe I should have stayed home with my ceiling cracks. At least in bed I could curl up into a ball without anyone noticing.

"Eva?" says a voice, a real voice…I'm pretty sure. "*Evaaaa…*" The voice stretches out my name like taffy. I slide my noise-canceling headphones off and swivel in my chair to find Margie standing stooped, weight shifted to one hip reluctantly. There's a smattering of worry sheetrocked poorly across her brow. "Did you finish that newsletter?" she asks, but only after I've been staring at her so long that it forces her hand.

SHIVA

My head bobs up and down. "Yeah. Didn't I send it to you?"

"It's not in my inbox."

I check my computer. The e-mail had been typed but saved in drafts. I click on *edit*, check the content, and send it over to her. "Done," I chirp, giving her a smile that feels too wide. Too forced.

The intention of the smile was to send Margie away but it has the opposite effect. She frowns and asks the question I'd been trying to prevent everyone from asking. "Do you need a break?" The words leave her mouth softly like the rustling of parchment paper. The kind you stick in the oven. "If you need some air or something, don't be afraid to take it."

Time. Air. Things my dumbass brother no longer has. The last thing I need is an excess of either. I shrug in a noncommittal way which will hopefully appease us both. "Thanks, maybe later." With that I turn back to my computer, staring at the screen and revisiting tasks I finished not ten minutes before until she gives up and goes away.

No time. No air. Just work. I need work.

THOMAS

RAIDING A DEAD woman's kitchen makes you feel like an asshole, but it's not like dead women eat. Evie's got all this cereal. Snacks. A carton of milk that's only just a few days expired. The fridge at my place has a burrito I waited too long to finish. It's green now. It was not green when I bought it.

After the blonde showered and left, I poured myself some Lucky Charms and sat on the couch watching the place where a television would be if Evie had ever bothered to own a television. She was weird like that. Or maybe there's one in the bedroom. I don't know. I haven't made it back there yet. Right now, I'm up to my third bowl of Lucky Charms and already my tongue is coated in that stale, sugary, milky aftertaste you always get with cereal. I should probably stop eating it, this stuff will give me the shits, but if I stop then I have to start going through her things. There's no way I'm ready for that. Nope. I'd rather shit rainbows.

The way the sun is coming into the apartment suggests mid-afternoon but I haven't bothered to confirm it. I just keep on eating my cereal and watching the TV that isn't there and wondering where the closest liquor store is in proximity to this apartment. With my luck, it's probably at least a mile. She would have done that intentionally as to not tempt herself. Her and her fucking self-control. It almost makes me angry, not because she was good and I was bad but because she's not here to benefit from being good and her absence is now making everything I do feel even badder.

I spoon some sugar-soaked milk into my mouth before abandoning the empty bowl on the table and leaning back on the couch. It's quiet here, especially for a building on a busy street. She liked the quiet, probably would have moved out to the middle of fucking nowhere if she wasn't so worried about bears. And bees. And everything else the great outdoors had to offer that indoor cat of a woman. Because that's what she was: an indoor cat. Keeping to herself. Hissing at anyone who might want to get close. Not that you can blame her. The only tie she kept was to me. And I'm the sonofabitch that killed her.

EVA

WATCHING THE TIME on my computer go from four fifty-nine to five o'clock usually sends a rush of relief through my entire body, like a big breath after swimming too long underwater. Today, it didn't feel like anything, and as five-o-one rolls around, my stomach lurches.

So, I don't take the bus home. Instead, I walk. It's at least a forty-minute walk but it gives me time to think—or, more precisely, time to avoid thinking entirely. The world can shift and slide around me as it will. No need to stop or pay attention. Just one foot in front of the other. Over and over.

Unfortunately, I haven't done a lot of walking since the accident—and if I'm being honest, since way before the accident. Exercise isn't really my thing. It moves too fast. Twenty minutes in and I'm sweating, the back of my neck so damp I must look like an out-of-breath chain smoker attempting a 5k. I can't take my jacket off because the weather is still too crisp and so I continue at an increasingly lethargic pace, slowly cooking from the inside out.

SHIVA

When I finally reach home, you could stick a fork in me. I climb the steps up to the oh-so-far-away second floor, stop in the hallway, and breath heavily. I should probably get back into shape—or *in* shape, given that I've never really been in shape to begin with. Fumbling in my deep, cozy coat pocket, I retrieve my keys and head for the door.

I unlock it, open it, and—

For a hairline of a second, there he is. My brother on the couch.

I flip the light on to get a better look and as a florescent glow illuminates the room, he vanishes. A shiver courses through my body, as warm and sticky as I feel. I step back out into the hall, close the door. Wait a beat. Hold my breath. Not sure what holding my breath will do exactly. It just feels appropriate. Almost like a prayer.

Then, I open the door again, expecting to see him sitting there. He isn't. Of course, he isn't. *Fuck*. I slam the door shut behind me, stare wide-eyed into the living room. Waiting. I'm not sure for what. For my brother to reappear? Or for him to pop up behind me like a funhouse clown? Before I turned the lights on, it had looked like he was lying there asleep on the couch. Asleep or—or dead. But then again, we can all look dead in the dark.

I drape my purse across the kitchen-table chair and slip off my coat. The room smells like it's been doused in gasoline, or maybe that's just the wires in my brain misfiring. It's tempting almost—the urge to say his name. Call it into the quiet and wait to see if anything calls back.

But what good could that do? After a few minutes I rub my face and head into the bathroom. The mirror above the sink reminds me that there's still a faint brown-green ring around my eye. I've never understood that. The more a bruise heals, the worse it looks somehow. I want a bath. And a drink. A muted evening wrapped up in the thick, tender haze of being too drunk to care. I'll get neither, of course. No alcohol for me, and when I'm sober, baths make me too fidgety to truly enjoy them. There are times when I'm certain that's what I miss most about drinking. Being drunk in the bath. It's dangerous of course—people have drowned that way—but it's part of the allure, to lie half sunken into oblivion. Warm and relaxed as the world moves on without you.

There are no sensations when you're dead, though. Afterlife is bullshit. Heaven, hell…all bullshit. There's nothing of you prior to your existence and nothing left of you once that existence has concluded. I know this to be true. I believe it—have always believed it—so why does the image of my brother on the sofa prickle at the back of my neck? A sensation I can recognize but not place—feel, but not quite reach out and touch. I exhale to empty out that gasoline taste.

"Hello?" I say aloud. The word falls from my lips like a shriveled petal.

There is no response because I am talking to the walls. It's so stupid I could scream, but then I'd just be screaming. And what's the point of that?

THOMAS

I WAKE UP on the couch to what sounds like Evie's voice. It's night, probably, or close enough to it. There's a marked pain in my neck. I notice it even before I'm fully awake and, sliding up onto my ass, I rub at the base of my skull with tired, nail-bitten fingers. However long I was lying at that twisted angle was too long. My neck is so knotted it won't even crack. I lean my head against the back of the couch and the front of my skull throbs.

Her voice still feels fuzzy in my ears, like wax half cleaned out. I listen like she might repeat herself, say something else, and when she doesn't a pang of guilt slithers through my rumbling gut. I need to eat something. Or puke. With this headache it's hard to tell which. Both maybe. But which one first?

Unable to decide, I opt for neither. Slump back down into a curled-up position and stare at the wall. I want another drink. I want another stranger's tongue in my mouth. I want a hot dog and ibuprofen and to leave my dead sister's shitty apartment and never look back.

There's that goddamn puzzle on the kitchen table, the

last one she'd been working on before the accident, and I haven't had a chance to look at it yet. In fact, I've avoided it entirely. Evie and her puzzles. She never had any interest in them when we were growing up—she started in college or after college. Whenever she got into therapy.

Suddenly, nausea floats to the top of my belly like a balloon. I can't remember the last time I puked and don't have time to figure it out. Shoving myself onto the floor, I rise to my feet and stumble towards the bathroom in anticipation of the absolute shitshow that is about to be unleashed.

I stop in front of the sink but instead of spewing everywhere I rock back and forth dreamily. There's nowhere to go and the jarringly surreal comprehension of this fact almost makes me forget the nausea. Forget what brought me in here.

There's no space to get to the toilet. She's blocking it.

Her name curls like smoke in the back of my throat. "Evie."

EVA

A SCREECH OF a squeal leaves my mouth, and as the sound peels away, the echo leaves something like a raw, dry husk in its wake.

Wake. Waking. Am I awake? Yes, at least I think so.

Before I can properly look into my dead brother's face he is gone and I am alone again the bathroom. Alone and suddenly feeling very exposed. I close the door, as if that might keep whatever I've just witnessed out, then decide against barricading myself in the shower and go back into the living room. "Thomas?" I call my brother's name into the empty room, this time genuinely expecting a response. "Thomas?"

I spin and spin and spin until I'm dizzy, but he's nowhere in sight. Thomas's soft warm eyes. They're unmistakable. Like teddy bear fuzz. Abruptly, my feet come to a halt. A gas leak. There must be a gas leak somewhere in the apartment and it's fucking with my brain. I go to the chair to grab my purse so I can call the building manager when I feel someone standing behind me. I don't know how I feel it or why I feel it, but I turn around.

There's no one there. Not a soul. But the smell of gasoline is back. Stronger, this time.

I go drop myself onto the couch—because my knees can no longer hold the weight of me—and stare into the blankness of the room. This is what madness looks like. Not feeling insane but experiencing things that feel so real you cannot help but believe them. Thomas was in my bathroom, then he was not. Thomas was dead, then he was not. But *he is* dead. I know that to be true. I have a black eye to prove it.

The concussion. Maybe this is all an effect of the concussion. Or the concussion knocked something loose and I'm having a brain aneurysm. How do brain aneurysms work again? I used to know. Used to google it and google it and slide down that self-diagnosis rabbit hole until I couldn't take it anymore and had to crack open a bottle of tequila. Even after what I had seen drinking do to my dad…to my brother's dad…to Thomas himself. Because the truth is that I was a shut-in who dropped sixty pounds in two months and was barely maintaining her grades and spending all of her time outside of class catastrophizing on the World Wide Web. Rabbit-holing was my only hobby senior year. And it nearly killed me. Until I started drinking. And then the drinking nearly killed me. And then I stopped all of it. Got my shit together. But it didn't matter. Because eventually Thomas's shit always becomes my shit. That's how it works.

Some time passes. I'm not sure how much. When my knees finally restore themselves, I get up and get my phone and call Francine.

DAY FIVE

THOMAS

"ANYTHING ELSE?" ASKS the girl behind the counter, weight to one hip and a single finger suspended above a button on the cash register. She has curves and dimples and a sleeve of tattoos unfurling from her shoulder to her wrist. I want to invite her back to my place. Evie's place. At the thought, a shiver slinks down my spine. Inviting women there should not be my default. "Anything else?" she asks again, brow slightly raised. She's not impatient yet, but if she has to say it again, she will be. I shake my head. She presses the button, bags the whiskey. "Twenty-two seventy-nine."

Walking out into an evening clad in streetlight, I wonder if I should crack the bottle open now. What if I don't and Evie's there when I get back. Or worse—what if I open it and I get back and she's there anyway? I pass a cop car parked by the curb and hug close to a brick wall as I turn the corner, cradling the paper bag close. Just holding that bag brings with it all the assurances of a done deal, an event that hasn't happened yet but has been set in motion and cannot be stopped. I will drink this. I will get back to

Evie's place and I will drink it and I will feel good and I will feel calm and I will fall asleep and when I wake up, I will feel like shit and nothing will have changed but that's the way it will be. Setting your mind on something is like jumping into a future where it's already happened and what you're experiencing in the present is a memory. A flesh-and-bone record of what cannot be changed.

It'll be fine. I was hungover yesterday. Seeing things after a few too many, it happens. Not to me. But—it must happen, right? People talk about it. At least I think they do. I haven't been to a meeting in a while, and even when I bothered to go, I didn't really pay much attention. But that's all right. I doubt they were listening to me either. Addiction makes us selfish, right? Isn't that the deal? That's what Evie used to tell me. But seeing things? Hell, people see things all the time. Or think they see things, anyway.

When we were kids, our youngest cousin on our mother's side had an imaginary friend named Herschel. She was six at the time and claimed Herschel was a seven-year-old boy in a white tunic. Everyone thought it was weird—would jokingly claim someone named Herschel must have died in the house a hundred years before even though no one really believed it. But what if they were right? What if it was as simple as that? Herschel was dead and what Josie thought was her friend was really his ghost. Josie doesn't remember Herschel anymore. That's the creepiest part.

We all remember Thanksgivings and Chanukahs and birthdays with her going on and on about his habits and interests and his allergy to strawberries. But ask her today and she will shrug like you've just said the name of a celebrity she's too young to remember. She doesn't have any idea what we're talking about, and if someone brings it up, she chews on the inside of her lip and grumpily tells us "enough with the fucking Herschel" like it's some

SHIVA 59

embarrassing blemish on her youth. What if Evie is my Herschel? Only, you don't get ghosts as an adult—do you? No. Of course not. Because you don't get ghosts, full stop, case in point, end of fucking sentence.

If someone were to haunt me though, it might as well be Evie. And I'd deserve everything she'd throw at me. No contest.

EVA

THERE'S NOTHING TO say except the truth, which is why I don't say it. My stasis is so prevalent I imagine the permanent indentation I must be making on Francine's sofa. Since my therapist retired, she's the only person I feel comfortable opening up to. "You really don't seem well at all," Francine posits after two or three or eight minutes of me not saying anything but not getting up and leaving either.

"I'm tired," I admit at last, which is true. I am tired and I must be very tired to be seeing what I think I'm seeing. "I want a drink."

The admission doesn't come with shame or guilt. Merely fatigue. Francine frowns. "What you're going through is hard."

Words pile up in my mouth. "It's not that—or it is that—or—or—I don't know. How am I even supposed to tell what is and isn't related to *what I'm going through*?"

I use air quotes there to minimize the gravity of the term's meaning and Francine isn't amused. She sighs. "Fuck it then. Take away what you're going through.

SHIVA 61

Throw it out. Get rid of it. What are you left with? What are you feeling?"

I don't know if I can separate them. Compartmentalizing has it's uses but it gives you gaps—spots you can't process and therefore can't interpret. It's not conducive to the large-scale overthinking my brain is wired to handle. "Nothing?" I say and it's a question not an answer.

Her lips purse. She nods. "Well, that's a start."

We talk for ten, maybe fifteen, minutes more before I make excuses. That used to be my go-to: giving in to impulses and then trying desperately to retract every move made thus far. I called Francine in a panic—made her see me in a panic—and now that I have her attention the only thing I want is to be alone again.

At the door she hugs me, holding my hands in hers as she draws away. "Not feeling is just as valid as feeling," she reminds me. "Sometimes you need to experience one and let it thaw to get the other."

Francine is the wise, good-natured, motherly figure I never expected to find. Maybe that's the real difference between my brother and me, when all is said and done. I found my Francine and he didn't find his. I replaced hating on myself so ardently with talking about it. And the talking helps. At least, it usually does. Only, the first easy breath I take is alone in Francine's hallway, her door shut and locked behind me. The hallway smells like staleness—like an empty classroom or a long-unused basement—but the quiet of it feels good all around me.

I take a few more deep, diligent breaths before heading downstairs and out into the frostbitten air. It's so crisp I can feel my cheeks chapping with the first lazy brush of icy wind. I wait for a light to change and move through the crosswalk with my arms folded flat against my chest—a stance most convenient for warmth even though it looks stony and that has a tendency to draw all the worst kinds of attention. A guy at the next corner starts calling at me from the wall he's using to keep himself propped up, an unlit cigarette poised like a pointer in his hand. He jabs it in my direction while I wait for this light to change. I try to tune it out—I try to tune everything out all the time—but words like "pretty" and "baby" and "smile" slip through the cracks in my resolve like sewer guck. I stiffen, cringe, and do my best not to look at him.

The light is taking a particularly long time to change and the longer I ignore him the more adamant he gets in his catcalling. "Baby…baby, do you hear me?" he goes on, and from the corner of my eye I can see that he is disengaging himself from the wall. Shit. *Shit.*

My weight shifts impatiently from one foot to the other.

He's close now. He was too close even over by the wall but he's definitely too close now. "*Baby, you should listen when someone's talking to you…*"

I can smell the nicotine as he brushes a blonde curl away from his eye, droning on about how women never listen anymore and are so rude and how he'd hoped I wouldn't be like other girls but clearly, I'm a stuck-up bitch like the rest of them.

It seems like he might be drunk, but I can't be certain, and when his hand finally moves for my arm, it is not his proximity but jealously over what I presume to be drunkenness that makes me whirl around on my heels.

The WALK light finally turns green. I punch him in the face.

THOMAS

SHE ISN'T HERE. Good.

I close the door with my heel and head straight for the couch. The paper bag slips to the floor as I pull the bottle out. I leave it there, because if she isn't here to haunt me then she won't be telling me to pick up after myself either. I place the bottle on the table and unwrap a burrito I grabbed at the bodega on the corner.

The smell of beans and cheese rises up, displacing the Eva-ness of the apartment. The whole place smells like her. I noticed it this morning. Stale and clean with a hint of sandalwood because she has like five unused candles lying all around the place. Obviously, that puzzle on the table doesn't actually smell like wet cardboard, but every time I look at it, I smell it anyway. So, I breathe in burrito steam. It's too hot to eat yet and I put it on the table (no napkin because who cares?) and unscrew the cap off the bottle. That *click* of the seal breaking. I like that sound.

It's funny, or not funny but sad or fucked up or whatever, that there are things we can go years and years without thinking about and then someone involved in one of those things dies and the memory of it jumps the queue. Evie doesn't—didn't—like burritos because when she was fifteen, I made her go on the Ferris wheel at our grandparents' local fair. This was maybe a year before I started with Dad's whiskey. So, she hated me, but the normal sister amount—not extra yet.

We'd just eaten but I told her the Ferris wheel was slow—it would be fine. She hadn't realized it was one of those Ferris wheels with the carriages that flip and I'd seen them but purposefully didn't say anything. Once we were up in the air, I started flipping our cart around, just for kicks. Like a little shit. Must've done it one too many times because Evie puked before we even got off the ride. Projectile vomited all over me, herself, the ride attendant, and three girls we didn't know as she scrambled to get out. They had to shut the Ferris wheel down to take care of the mess, and Evie, who'd eaten a bean burrito with extra cheese from the stand next to the fried dough cart, never forgave me—or the burrito—for the humiliation of it.

I take a sip and there is nothing more satisfying than that first gulp of whiskey after a long day. Or morning. Or whatever. I sit and soak in the sensation of it as it buzzes through my body, wait for the feeling to even out and then take another large swig. Evie didn't like whiskey. Or beer. Or anything normal people drink. Not that it mattered. She hadn't touched the stuff since they put her on the Prozac. Not that people don't drink on antidepressants. People do. All the time. Not Evie though. She wanted to follow the rules. Make the most of them. Before the pills though, before that, my sister was a tequila girl and not even in some kitschy way either. She'd drink it straight up. No shots. No mixed drinks. Just tequila in a fucking glass like she hated herself. Because she did. Or at least she hated me. So, she drank harder than I did. To prove she could. To make me look like the whiny little bitch. Not that it was a competition. Then again, for Evie, it probably was.

EVA

MY KNUCKLES STING, blushing red as if it were embarrassment and not the punch turning them a few shades past pink. I should ice them when I get home.

It's a strange thing, to hit someone. I'd never done it before. My brother had once or twice but that was exactly why I'd made sure never to lapse into the same self-indulgent self-destruction. I choose to combust in different ways. More manageable ways. The kind that involve jigsaw puzzles and egregiously polite emails and the counting of cracks in the ceiling paint.

A small silver sports car takes a turn too sharply, causing a mid-sized sedan to honk in return. My body tightens. That sound. When our car went spinning that day, everything snapped quickly into darkness, but when I regained consciousness that was the first thing I heard. The sound of the horn blaring. It was because Thomas was slumped over with his cheek flat down against the steering wheel, pressing into it. Making that sound carry on and on and on until it rang just as clearly inside my head as it did outside it. Thomas with his lip split in two and his eyes

SHIVA

open—not wide necessarily, but wide enough to be able to tell that those eyes of his couldn't see a damn thing. He was dead. When I woke up and the car was in the river and gasoline was leaking into the water, my brother was already dead.

I cross the street quickly. Eager, in spite of myself, to get back. Because there is safety in knowing. There is safety in my ceiling with those fifteen cracks. I count them with every step, visualize them in my head and am calmed by the sureness of them. The numbers hum in my brain like bees in a hive and I tell myself that as long as I can get back and check the ceiling and prove to myself that they are there, it will be all right. Everything will be all right.

Or it won't. Either way. It doesn't matter.

When I'm finally home, I drop everything on the chair by the kitchen table and walk into my room and fall across the bed, shoes still on my feet as I stare up unblinking at the ceiling. *One, two, three…*

I find those cracks. Seek them out slowly, registering the precise length and width of each one.

Four, five, six…

The room begins to feel like it's sliding, my eyes steeped in dizziness.

Seven, eight, nine, ten, eleven…

I sit up, craning my neck to get a better look.

Twelve, thirteen, fourteen…

That's when I feel it—the pitter-patter prickle of something on my shoulder.

Fifteen!

I tense, turn. And there's Thomas. This time he doesn't vanish, but he doesn't look quite right either. His presence feels like something shifting in and out of focus—not blurred, exactly, but inconstant. He says my name, at least I see him do so, but no sound emits from his lips. He says it again and I blink blankly like someone who has not yet come to terms with the fact that they are having a stroke.

When at last the word breaks through and I hear my name spoken aloud in his voice, not *Eva* as everyone has always called me but *Evie* which he'd nicknamed me as a child, the syllables feel like pressure in my ears waiting to pop. I reach out a hand to touch his shoulder, prove his realness, but can't quite bring myself to do it. "You're dead," I mutter in a soft, malleable tone. It is pliant like chocolate melting in the sun. His expression goes dark, his eyes hard but thinly so. My brother always had a gentle heart.

THOMAS

HER EXPRESSION IS calm and centered, with only tiny cracks in her composure. The kind you don't see if you're not looking. But I see them. The scrunch in the corner of her lip indicating that she's biting on the inside of her cheek. The slight crease in her forehead. "I saw you die," she continues.

"That's not how I remember it."

I know because I saw it myself. The life leaving her face. I watched while my head went spinning and sirens sounded somewhere in the distance, blood gurgling in her throat like she had something to say. Always having to get the last word in. Even as she…

Evie's hand is still partially raised like she might hug me. Hit me. I touch her arm and the fuzzy, worn-out polyester feels as real as my own skin. She jumps, a hiccup of an involuntary movement, then goes still again.

"You're dead," she repeats. Her voice is so strained. Her brain must be spiraling.

"No." I shrug sheepishly. Defensively. Drunkenly. "You are."

It's like we're teenagers again fighting over who started shoving who first while Mom hollered for both of us to be quiet, turned the radio up so she wouldn't have to listen to us. I could go on, tell Evie how I know she's dead, but explaining to her what I've done and what it did to her isn't something I'm eager to do. The silence flattens between us.

"You think I'm…" Her words falter, like she's failing to grasp a complicated math problem posed in a classroom. She doesn't quite understand it, she doesn't even see the merit of understanding it, but she's trying. I nod and she frowns. This is the Evie I remember. The sister who needs the world ordered in the boxes she's organized herself. The one who has to understand everything about everything, no matter the price.

EVA

"ONE OF US is wrong," I say in a voice meant to sound reassuring, except there's nothing reassuring about the words once I hear them out loud. If this were any other situation, Thomas probably would have laughed at them.

Instead, he shrugs again. "Or both of us are right."

"No. We'd remember it the same then, wouldn't we?"

He doesn't say a word. His fingers are fidgety. He wants a drink. I know because I do too. Desperately. Our mother had ended things with his father for the same reason she'd ended things with mine: The man drank too much. Lo and behold, she bore each of them a child marked by the very same affliction. Our mother, like so many mothers, deserved better than what she got. But what we want and what we want to want are hardly ever the same. She wanted them. She wanted us. And look where that led us. I think about the cracks on the ceiling above us. Wish I could count them without him noticing. "One of us is imagining this," I decide.

"Or we're still dying," he says. "Maybe this is our brains—what do you call it? Shutting down? Signals firing at random while we die…"

A laugh escapes me this time, not because what he's saying is funny but because he's saying it with a practical seriousness that is so unlike him. Maybe I'm the dead one. Maybe I'm the dead one and I'm just imagining a half-assed phantom of Thomas.

"What?" he asks, nose wrinkling. Not like I've offended him but like he doesn't get the joke.

The urge to touch his shoulder strikes me and my hand lurches forward, then wilts. What if it wakes one of us up? Fingers tense like twigs about to snap, I perch them on the sleeve of his t-shirt and wait for the world to unravel around us.

Only, there is no great undoing. No instant of revelation. All I feel is cotton and the curve of his shoulder beneath it. My fingers withdraw quickly and he flinches. He's real. Does that mean I'm not? "Did you feel my hand?" I ask.

He nods. Shoves sheepishly at my arm. "You feel that?" he asks.

This time I nod, and for a good long while, or at least what feels like a good long while but in actuality is probably only a moment or two, neither of us says anything. The silence gives me time to smell the whiskey on him. Underneath it though—underneath it there's still that stench of gasoline.

He must notice as the whiskey hits me because he shrugs and pushes his hands deep into his pockets. "Might've fallen off the wagon…"

"Looks like after you fell it doubled back and ran you over."

He smirks, shakes his head like I wouldn't understand. Except we both know I do. "So, you've been perfect since I supposedly died. Not affected at all?"

"I didn't say that."

"You're not drinking."

SHIVA

Maybe it's because he's right. Or maybe it's because I'm talking to my dead brother. Either way, I turn around.

"Where are you going?" he calls as I leave the room. "Evie?"

He follows after, I can hear him, but I ignore his questions as I check the counter, cabinets, under the sink. "Where is it?" I ask him bluntly. This time he's the one who doesn't answer and so I look up to see the dark, hollow, guilty shadows beneath his eyes. It's then I notice it on the table behind him, and so I march into the living room and take his whiskey bottle and unscrew the cap.

"Evie…" he protests. Because my brother will challenge me to anything so long as he's sure I won't actually do what he's daring me to do. "Evie, wait a minute—"

I look him in the eye, so he knows I'm doing this for him—fucking myself up for him. That's the way it's always been. He looks like absolute shit as I raise the bottle to my lips and take an unforgiving gulp. I expect the burn. That beautifully wretched smart which comes with the release of giving in. But that's not what happens.

The whiskey tastes like nothing. It tastes like water.

Scrutinizing the bottle in my hand, I tilt my head. "What did you put in this?"

His brow knits. "Huh?"

"This isn't alcohol."

He grabs the bottle from me, takes a quick sip. Shakes his head. "It's definitely alcohol." When I move to retrieve the bottle—to try again—his pulls it from my reach with the protective air of a father guarding a child. My look must go mean, because he shrugs. "If you can't taste it anyway…"

He's right. I can't taste it. The bottle is his, not mine. Suddenly, I get an idea. And I'm off again. This time Thomas doesn't bother tailing me. He just sits down on the couch, making himself comfortable as he takes another drink. I return with a cardboard box and drop it onto the living room floor dramatically.

"What's that?"

"Your shit," I reply. Because unlike him, I actually went to his apartment and cleared everything out after he died—I'd had to—and now the culmination of his entire life is taking up room in my closet. I open the box and rummage through until I find what I'm looking for: a joint he'd left in a jacket pocket. I hold it up for him to see like it's the Grail. I return to the box for a lighter and, upon retrieving one, bring both over to the couch.

"You don't smoke," he says as I light up the joint.

"No, but you do."

With that I hold it out for him, smoke swirling up from the tip. For a moment it looks like he might argue, but he doesn't. Because Thomas never turns down a drink. Or a hit. Or anything anyone goes through the trouble to put directly in front of him.

THOMAS

THE TASTE IS so stale it's practically nonexistent. No. It *is* nonexistent. I look up at Evie, who is now watching with wide, impatient eyes and tense hands perched on her knees. I look down at the rolled paper between my fingers and sniff at it. "What is this?"

"It's your pot."

"Bullshit."

"I swear" she says, taking the joint from my hand and bringing it to her lips. She inhales, then chokes so hard she nearly drops the thing on the floor and I have to free it from her hands, stub it out on the heel of my shoe. There's a cloud of smoke hovering between us but it doesn't smell like smoke. It smells like that stuff dry ice gives off—a smell that is a little off but essentially odorless. Her eyes are glassy as she blinks up at me, regaining her composure. "*Trust me…*" she wheezes out, clearing her throat. I don't think Evie's smoked a day in her life and the temptation to see her high is almost outweighed by the point of her experiment.

"So, what?" I ask. "I can't mess with your stuff and you can't mess with mine?"

She leans back, rests her head against the back of the couch, her neck crooked to one side. "It would appear so."

"What about the floor?" I continue, gesturing towards out feet. "Or the couch?"

"They exist in both your version and in mine." She shrugs. "But the whiskey is only here because you brought it here, and that box is only here because I took it from your place after you…" Her voice falters and she doesn't finish the sentence.

"After we died," I say for her.

Her expression hardens. "We can't both be dead."

"Why not?"

"Because even our family isn't that fucked."

EVA

WE'VE BEEN SILENT for some time now, Thomas only moving to take another drink from the whiskey bottle. Having none myself, I reclaim the joint he placed on the table and light it up again. "You don't smoke," he chimes lazily, not looking up as I try to stifle the havoc swirling in my lungs. I lean back on the sofa, closing my eyes and exhaling towards the ceiling. My brother is sprawled at the other end of the couch, his head against the armrest as he drinks and sighs and drinks some more. He sounds like a bored housewife and I start to giggle. "What?" he says, this time glancing my way.

"I don't know which is weirder," I reply. "This"—I gesture between the two of us, our present little bonding sesh—"or *this*"—I gesture widely to encompass the whole room, the situation we've found ourselves in.

He slouches up a little, the half-empty bottle cradled between his body and the cushion. "Definitely this," he says, pointing between me and him. Because of course. Defying the laws of time and space, that's one thing. But a Drucker-Mahone family reunion: unprecedented. Even in an alternate reality where one of us is dead and the other is experiencing some kind of psychotic break. "Was there a funeral?" he asks suddenly. The question doesn't have any eagerness or weight to it. I nod without a word. "Anyone show?" he continues, that same matter-of-factness in his tone.

"Of course."

He snorts.

"What?"

"You say *of course* like I'm a jackass for asking."

"You are a jackass for asking."

I take another hit and again try not to choke. It's getting a little easier now.

Through the haze I see him half grin, half smirk. "You're not going to ask, are you?"

"Ask what?"

"About yours."

"You actually had one?"

"Jesus Christ, Evie!"

I sit up, stubbing out the joint because I can tell I've already smoked too much and it's turned my head into a warm, woolly space devoid of pretense. A chuckle escapes my throat. "What does Jesus Christ even mean to Jews anyway?"

"Can we go back to you assuming I wouldn't give you a funeral."

"I mean, it's not exactly a birthday party," I spit.

"You sound annoyed."

"I'm not annoyed"—*lie*—"I'm just tired of this."

"Tired of what?"

"This. You. Me. Just—*everything*."

"Well, it's a good thing you're dead then" he says, freezing as he says it.

THOMAS

SHE'S MAD. AND freaked. Even if she's pretending not to be. Or maybe she's just being Evie. At this point, who can even tell?

"Right," she says, rising sharply and unsteady on her feet. "I want tequila. And disco fries."

"You don't drink."

She waves without looking at me, grabbing her purse off the kitchen chair. "Doesn't count if I'm already dead."

I say nothing as she slams the door behind her and go for another sip, but the bottle is empty. If I call her phone, will she hear it? Would she answer if she did? According to Evie's dead man's logic, I wouldn't be able to drink the whiskey even if she brought it back for me. Maybe I can DoorDash or Uber Eats something to the apartment. But I don't feel like getting up. Or looking for my phone or wasting time or thinking more than is absolutely necessary about any one thing. Maybe I'm better at this being dead stuff than I would have expected.

Maybe Evie was right and I deserve everything I get. I slump down on the couch. Sip at my empty bottle just out of habit and wait for her to come back.

But what if she doesn't? What if that was it? I saw my dead sister for five minutes and the last thing we talked about was disco fries. *Fuck*. It should bother me, but that pit grumbling in my stomach is really hunger. I'm hungry. And I need more whiskey. I pull myself up off the couch slowly, like I'm moving through wet sand, and find my phone on the counter. I pull up a menu for the closest pizza place—because Evie is sure to have cash lying around here somewhere—and call for delivery. A pepperoni pizza with peppers and a Coke because pizza joints don't stock whiskey. The girl on the phone says thirty-five minutes and I wonder if Evie will be back before the food gets here. What if she is? Will whoever delivers the pizza see her? Or is my dead sister haunting only me?

The rules of it all make my head hurt. Or maybe that's just the whiskey. *Fuck*. I should just walk down to the liquor store. Pick the pizza up on the way. What the hell else is there to do?

EVA

THE SMELL OF cheese and gravy rising from the paper bag beneath my arm is enough to make my head spin. With my free hand, I dig around for the keys in my purse until I remember that I didn't lock the door when I left. Why would I? My brother was there. Only, he couldn't have been.

I try the handle and the door falls open slowly. The apartment is empty. *I was hallucinating. Shit.* It should be a relief but there's disappointment snagged in the gratitude. It was imaginary. All of it. Am I having a breakdown? Is that what this is? I'm not sure I even care at this point. I just want my goddamn fries.

Suddenly, the door to the stairway opens and I hear slow, lazy footsteps on the hallway carpet. My body tenses. I turn around and there he is. Thomas. He's holding a pizza box and a brown paper bag under his arm. He shrugs. "I was hungry."

I'd hate him if only I could stop loving him. That's the worst thing about my brother. I love him even when I shouldn't—even when it's in my best interest not to. Even when one—or both—of us is dead.

We enter the apartment like it's the most natural thing in the world—like one or the other or both of us isn't probably dead—and I close the door behind us. Lock it for safe measure, lest any other deceased relatives try to join us. Mom maybe. Or one of our dads. *For fuck's sake, could you imagine?* Dread pools in my gut like bile.

"Antonio's?" I ask, eyeing the pizza.

"I guess."

"The place on the corner?"

He nods.

That's Antonio's. My favorite pizza joint in all of Jersey, actually. Not that I intend to try his. I can't imagine what tasteless cheese feels like on the tongue. He places the pizza on the counter, slides down the edges of the paper bag to reveal a fresh bottle of whiskey. "Didn't see you at the liquor store," he says, eyeing my own bag.

"Must've missed you."

He balls up the paper bag to his bottle and tosses it in the trash. I don't move from my spot by the door. "Jose Cuervo?"

"Patrón."

He smirks. "You were always picky."

I put my fries on the counter and unwrap my bottle of Patrón, let the paper fall to the floor, and hold the tequila to my chest as I make my way to the couch. He watches wordlessly as I struggle with the cork, finally pull it loose, and take a swig. It burns like the voice of God. A thrill extends through my body—a jolt as dopamine rushes my brain in a dizzying wave. I lower the bottle to my lap and look up to see my brother making a scrunched-up, little-boy face of disgust. The first time he ever got drunk was on tequila. He hates the stuff. I pull a deep breath and take another sip, just to disgust him, before putting the cork back in and resting the bottle on the coffee table. I

SHIVA

rise to my feet and a rush fizzles in the pit of my stomach.

Thomas scratches as his chin, averting his eyes as I go to the counter. Without a word I pop open the Styrofoam container holding my fries and pluck one from the steaming pile of gravy goodness. He waits until I'm chewing to ask: "When was the last time you did this?"

I think about the cracks in my bedroom ceiling, but they feel blurry and far away. I gaze at him wordlessly, mouth full of potato mush. He shakes his head and attends to his pizza. Pepperoni and peppers. Some things never change. "Where's the Coke?" I ask. As a kid, my brother never ate pizza without a Coke.

Having already taken a bite from his first slice, he wipes the grease from his lip. "They were out."

THOMAS

WE EAT AND drink in silence. You'd think we'd have more to talk about, but this is the way it's always been between us. Quiet, until it's not. Boring, until it's not. Mom used to call our silences the "eye of the storm." Within five minutes of her saying this, Evie and me were usually at each other's throats. Not normal brother and sister shit, either. There were times we really hated each other, would have wished the other out of existence if we had the chance. I guess some wishes come true.

She's not pacing herself. She's drinking too fast. Proof she hasn't had a drink in a good long while. I don't say anything about it because that would only send her into the opposite direction and encourage her to drink more. She probably thinks I like punishing her, but not in that way. It's not fun to watch someone hurt themself. Especially just for sport.

She's swirling a fry across the bottom of the Styrofoam to scoop up leftover gravy. Those things are gross. Gravy is basically meat sludge. But Evie loves her fat-soaked vegetables. As a kid, the only way to get her to eat her greens was to fry and bread them before putting any on her plate. My dad used to say you could fuel a pickup truck for a week on the garbage Evie ate.

"Stop it," she says suddenly. I look up and she's not watching me, she's still too focused on her fries, but as she pops another one into her mouth, I'm certain I heard what I thought I'd heard. It's creepy as fuck when she does that. Talks like she can see the inside of my head.

I start licking cheese grease from my fingers. "What?"

"Whatever you're thinking about, just stop it."

"How do you know what I'm thinking?"

"I don't. But when you get all quiet like that…it's never anything but trouble."

Evie tosses her empty container on the coffee table, sinks into the sofa, and hugs the tequila to her belly. She burps and it's so un-Evie-like I can't help but snicker.

She turns and looks directly at me. "What was my cause of death?"

Her expression is so matter-of-fact. So practical. I stop laughing. She waits and when I say nothing, her eyes widen impatiently. She won't let this go. It's clear by the look on her face.

"It was a car accident," I tell her.

"Yeah, so was yours, but—like—*how* did I die?"

"I don't want to tell you that."

"Why not?"

"It's…"

"What?" She's the one snickering now. "*Personal?*"

"I was gonna say fucked up."

"All of this is fucked up."

"What good will knowing do?"

"What good is not knowing doing me?"

Fuck. She's impossible. I clear my throat, try not to look at her. Suddenly, I feel too drunk. Or too sober. I can't tell which. "We went over the railing into the river and…and next thing I knew, there was…" My voice goes hoarse. I clear my throat. Without the whiskey in me I doubt I'd be able to get any of this out. "There was broken glass sticking out of your…you know, sticking"—I don't want to picture it but I can't not picture it—"um…sticking out of your, uh, your neck." Saying these things is like ripping fresh stitches out. "I only saw it for a second before it turned the water red so fast. Afterwards they said the shard must've hit an artery."

I can feel her eyes boring into me as she takes this information in. She exhales and I imagine her fingers going to her neck—trying to see if she can find where the artery would be on her own. I don't know what to tell her. There was so much blood at the time, I don't even remember which side of her neck it had been.

She shifts her weight on the couch. "Do you wanna know how you—"

"No."

The word spits out quiet but fast. It renders her silent immediately. Good. At least there's that. Head lowered, I raise my eyes to catch a glimpse of her. She looks frustrated, but when she speaks the words come out smooth. "Okay," she says. "We don't have to talk about it."

It's a relief—really, it is. But as the silence falls in icy sheets around us it becomes clear that there's nothing else to talk about. The realization seems to hit us around the same time and Evie takes a swig from her tequila bottle, probably because she can't sit still. I drink my whiskey, eyeing the unfinished puzzle she left on the kitchen table.

"Maybe this is purgatory," she says then.

"Do Jews believe in purgatory?"

She shrugs. "Maybe we have too much unfinished business and God won't let us leave until we've sorted it out."

SHIVA

"You don't believe in God."

She looks at me. Unfocused. Or maybe I'm the one with double vision at this point. It's hard to tell. I'm definitely too drunk. Not too sober. "Neither do you."

"Yeah, but I'm not the one talking about…" Saying the word *God* out loud again tastes wrong so I nod towards the ceiling, as if the very idea of a god might be lurking up there like a poltergeist. Those are the loud ghosts, right? Poltergeists? What's-his-name made a movie about them and Steven Spielberg produced it. Evie loved *E.T.* when we were little but that little alien dude freaked me the fuck out.

Acid reflux gurgles in my throat. I wash it down with more whiskey. "Do you think we have to see to all our unfinished business?" she asks. "Or…just…like, one fundamental thing that made us bad people."

"We weren't bad people."

"We weren't good people."

"Yeah, but *bad* and *not good* aren't the same thing."

She looks like she might laugh, but doesn't. "How would you know?"

It's impossible to talk about anything with her. Either Evie thinks you don't know what you're talking about or she thinks you want to pick it apart, examine every inch of the problem like it's a colonoscopy. She can't just let things be. "Fine, Evie. We're in purgatory."

"Why do you have to say it like that?"

"Like what?"

"Like it's such a ridiculous idea."

"It's not—it's just—I just don't think it matters, okay?"

She's staring at me. I can tell. And so I do my very best not to look at her. "I didn't sit shiva for you," she says quietly.

"So? I didn't for you either."

"Mom used to say it was bad luck not to sit shiva."

"Mom told us that so we wouldn't play video games after Grandpa's funeral."

Evie's lips purse together, jaw set tight. "Didn't work. We played video games anyway."

DAY SIX

EVA

DRY MOUTH AND sunshine on my face. These are the only sensations I can register upon waking—followed swiftly by the pounding in my skull that makes it feel as if a thousand spiders are burrowing into my brain. Sitting up would probably make me puke and so I don't. I wait. As if that will somehow suspend time and keep this hangover from taking full effect.

With reluctance I open my eyes to see the cracks spread out across my ceiling, old and familiar and safe. *Maybe getting drunk with my dead brother was a hallucination, after all.* Only, it wasn't. Because through the open doorway and down the hall I can see Thomas standing in my kitchen, refrigerator door open. He's just taken a swig of milk (expired milk?) directly from the carton. There's something hardwired into brothers that makes them do this. Drink from the carton. Double-dip their spoons. Once I even caught Thomas using my toothbrush because he didn't have one and wasn't going to go down the street to buy one. *Goddamn brothers.*

Thomas hasn't seen me yet and so as the refrigerator door closes, I roll over onto my side, press my cheek into the pillow, and close my eyes. Pretend to be asleep. I'd love to go back to sleep right now. For all the good it would do.

I don't hear him come up to the door but I do hear the creak as he leans against the doorframe. "Morning, sunshine."

In lieu of telling him to fuck off I merely groan.

"It's a good thing you're already dead," he says. "I don't think a living liver could have handled what you did to yourself last night."

At this, I sit up fast—too fast—and it's like being shoved underwater by a wave. "I'm not dead."

He waits a beat. Frowns. "Have you looked in the mirror?"

That underwater sensation is building—intensifying—and with it the current of consciousness is making me too dizzy. I struggle with the tangled sheets, shove past my brother and into the bathroom where I barely make it to the toilet before puking tequila and gravy and self-loathing so far above the bowl that it splashes the seat and the inside of the lid. The smell of it all entices more vomit to rise in my throat and the contents of my stomach empty in a slow, steady routine of retching and gasping and feeling every muscle in my body constrict and retract in unison.

Eventually, the internal spasming subsides and I fall onto my ass, back against the wall, legs stretched out across the tiled floor in front of me. I lean forward, flush the toilet, and realize that my head hurts just as much—if not more—than it did when I first woke up. *Fuck*.

I'm so hungover I'm shaking—physically shaking—and I look down at my trembling hands in dismay. The skin beneath the nail on my left index finger has a purplish hue to it—like a door must've closed on it or something and left a dark bruise. I poke at it with my other hand, but the pain it elicits is more than I was expecting and I hurl myself back at the toilet bowl to begin retching all over again.

THOMAS

EVIE LOOKS SMALL curled up in a ball on the floor like that. She's always been a large presence—a full presence—but doubled over with slicked back hair and her knees tucked beneath her, she looks like a little girl lost at sea.

I don't say anything while she throws up—there's nothing worse than someone trying to talk to you while you're puking. Except maybe having that someone be a brother you say is dead. Still, I don't need her fury directed at me. I'm more than happy to let the toilet take some of that wrath for a while. It's not even like I can make her some eggs or anything. This is why you've got to pace yourself though. Sure, my head feels like a meat cleaver has gone clear through it, but at least I'm not barfing like a thirteen-year-old after stealing their parents' wine coolers.

If I could feel sorry for her, I would. But that wouldn't do anyone any good. Besides, when was the last time Evie gave a shit about me? I can't remember. Or I don't want to remember. Maybe there's less difference between those two than you'd think. I don't know. "You need anything?" I ask at least. Because there's nothing else to be said.

She peers up at me with those big eyes that look like they are about to crack like glass in freezing temperatures. Impossible. She's always been impossible. She flushes the puke down the toilet, leans with her back against the wall. Breathing real fast like she might have a panic attack.

It happened a few times in college, according to Mom. Once, I even saw it happen. But I was under the impression she hadn't experienced one of these in a good, long time. She's trembling, but when I take a step in her direction, her body goes still. "Evie—"

She practically barks her response. "*No.*"

"What?"

"Just…" Her voice is shaking and her body quickly falls back in step. "Just—turn around or something. You look smug."

"I'm not smug."

"Go…away."

I don't do as she says and honestly, I can't tell if it's because I actually want to help or because she is the one telling me to do it. *Obstinate.* That's what she always calls me. The word sounds like a type of rock. Once I looked up what it meant but I don't remember it now. Just that it was her word for me. *Asshole* and *dumbass* and *little shit* being her favorite alternatives.

She isn't looking at me anymore, she's staring off at a fixed point in the bathroom. The door or the handle or the towel rack. It's hard to tell. But she's staring with the intensity one of the X-Men might use to move something with their mind. Who is the obstinate one really? Me or her?

Slowly, her breathing steadies. I don't even notice until suddenly I can't hear those sharp inhales and exhales anymore. I look back at her, half expecting her to have disappeared, but she's right there, poking at one of her fingernails apprehensively.

Without a word, I go back to the couch and pass out.

EVA

"WHAT'S THE MATTER?"

He's hunched forward over the sink, poking at his right eye with one finger. When he looks at me, I can see what he sees: The white of that eye is lined with burst blood vessels—like tiny, delicate red cracks in porcelain.

"What the fuck?" I move towards him, but he pulls away.

"It's fine."

"It's not fine—what the fuck is wrong with your eye?"

Thomas averts his stare to avoid answering and in doing so notices my fingernails. After he left me alone, three of them came off, loose and bloody like baby teeth. I put Band-Aids over all of them but now four more of my fingernails are beginning to look bruised. I curl my hands into fists and he looks up at me—one bloodied eye and one clear eye, each perfectly still as the line of his mouth squirms.

I'm itching for the imperfections in the bedroom ceiling—desperate to count them. I begin to picture the first one in my head. Long, like a taut spider leg pulled loose from the body. Before I can get to the second, Thomas raises his t-shirt to reveal discolored bruising across his abdomen. Purple and green and yellow blotches roughly the shape of Australia and just as big. "What the hell did you do to yourself?"

"Nothing. I woke up and it was just…just there. Same as the eye."

I turn around and pull at the neck of my shirt to reveal the bruise I noticed across my shoulder. "I thought I must've hit it last night…but…"

He's scared. Thomas gets so very rigid when he's scared. Almost like a deer or some other prey animal that knows it's seconds away from being mauled out of existence. At this, fear prickles like a series of hypodermic needles at the inside of my skin.

"I told you," he says. "We're dead."

This time I don't argue. I'm not entirely sure he's wrong, but I can't wrap my head around it being true either. I look down at my hands. Up at my brother. More than anything, I want to scramble into the other room and count my ceiling cracks. He says something else but I don't heart it and by the time I refocus to listen he is staring at me expectantly. "What?"

"This is only going to get worse. Isn't it?"

I don't answer again, which at this point is as good as agreeing with him. Without uttering a word, I go out into the bedroom—working hard not to glance up at the ceiling—and grab the near-empty tequila bottle off the floor. Take a gulp, emptying it.

It burns. But not in the way it should—that sharp, alcohol way. It burns like something hot and molten ripping through my chest. I drop the bottle and it shatters on the floor. Before I can make to the bathroom, I vomit not fresh tequila but blood onto the hardwood. I spit a few times to get the metallic taste out of my mouth, wipe my lips on the back of my hand. A smear of red blushes against the skin.

When I look up, Thomas is in the doorway. He's staring at the blood and broken glass on the floor but as soon as he realizes I'm watching him his attention snaps in my direction. Taking deep, stinging breaths, I look up at the ceiling in an attempt to find a crack—but my focus is fuzzy. I can't see straight. I can't—I can't—I can't—

THOMAS

IF SHE'D FALLEN forward, she would have landed on broken bottle shards, but instead she tilted back—hitting the back of her head on the nightstand as she fell to the floor. I can't tell which outcome would have been better. "Evie..." I'm whispering, which is dumb. Like I'm afraid to wake her. Or afraid that even if I start shouting, she still won't wake. The closer I get, the more that smell of dirty river water fills my nose. "Evie...Evie...look at me..."

Long-lashed lids flutter open as her eyes slip back in her skull. I pat her cheek like you see them do on TV, and slowly her eyes stop their rolling around and I think maybe she can see me.

"*Evie!*" I practically scream into her face. She stops blinking so much and I can tell as her eyes go into focus.

Her face twists up disapprovingly. "What are you looking at?"

"You passed the fuck out."

"No, I didn't."

"You're on the floor."

"No, I'm…" The word *not* gets stuck in her throat as she realizes where she is. She pulls herself up, leaning away when I try to help, and rests her head on the wall. She blinks again. "How long was I out?"

"Not long."

"It's getting worse."

"What is?"

She looks at me long and hard. It's the same look she gave me when I showed up that day asking for her help. "One of us must be dead," she says flatly.

"Why not both of us?"

She frowns. "I don't think this would be happening if we were both dead. One of us isn't supposed to be here."

EVA

HE CAN'T SEE it. Can't grasp the scope. Even though it was his guess in the first place. We've fucked with something. Glitched in a way the matrix of humanity just can't handle. One of us is supposed to be dead. We shouldn't be seeing each other. Talking to each other. It's like reality has split, but a split existence isn't sustainable. Maybe if one of us goes, all of this will stop.

I think about the ceiling in my room. How badly I want to go and lie down on the bed and count the cracks in the paint. Apply the certainty of them to my insides like a balm. But when I try to stand, dizziness floods my vision and I fall back down again. I'm so tired. Sleep tugs at the back of my brain. Or maybe that's the head wound.

When I look back at Thomas, his nose is bleeding. I say nothing and point. He reaches to touch his face and when he draws his fingers away, he sees the blood on his fingertips—stares as if he's not quite sure what he's seeing. I should have sat shiva for him. Maybe if I had, this wouldn't be happening. "You're right," he says. "It's getting worse. So, what do we do about it?"

"I honestly don't know."

"You said one of us is dead."

I nod.

"Which one?"

"It—I don't know. I'm not sure it matters. But one of us should be dead."

He leans back, his shoulders resting against the wall behind him as his sneakers slide him into a sitting position on the floor. He wipes his bloody nose on the back of his hand, but all it does is smear the red, causing the blood to cover twice as much surface space on his face as before. He sighs and it's a sigh I've always hated. A self-pitying useless sigh. Poor Thomas. Always poor fucking Thomas. He looks up at me then. "One of us needs to die again," he says matter-of-factly. Almost as if what he's suggesting is a normal part of growing up—like buying a car or showing up for jury duty. "That's what you mean."

My mouth opens. I don't speak. Because he's right. And there's no use arguing it.

"What if one of us just leaves? Goes far away?"

"I don't think proximity is the issue."

His eyes are open. Innocent. "Why not?"

"Because one of us is supposed to be dead."

"But what if we're wrong?" he asks. "What if one of us offs ourself and nothing changes for the other person?"

"There's only one way to find out."

He laughs. No. Cackles. He cackles like I've told some raunchy, twisted joke that proves I'm fucked up in the head. Maybe I am at this point. Maybe we both are. Both always were, even. Not that it would matter now.

His fit continues until he starts to choke. It takes him a minute or two to clear his throat enough to breathe and when he does he spits out a wad of blood. Not slick blood. But a clump. Almost like it had half congealed inside his body and gotten lodged there. He stares at it on the floor, his eyes slowly sobering. When he looks at me again, he does not resemble Thomas at all. "I'll do it," he says. "It should have been me anyway. It was my fault."

THOMAS

"ABSOLUTELY NOT." SHE barks. Because even when Evie thinks she's being protective, she's still a bully. "Out of the question."

"So you're volunteering?"

She bites her lip so hard I half expect it to split like tissue paper. "Maybe there's something else we can try first," she suggests. And that right there is the problem-solver I remember. The Evie I've always known and occasionally loved. I'd smile if the muscles in my face didn't feel like they were on fire.

"Like what?" I ask.

"I don't know. Anything. I mean, what you're suggesting should be the last resort, right? Not the first fucking option."

I shrug. Things can always get worse. She should know that. But who the hell am I to argue with my goddamn speeding train of a sister? Still, I don't feel like putting in the effort right now. And she looks like she's in even worse shape than me. "Can you stand?" I ask.

She places the palms of her hands on the floor, pushing herself up with the fragility of a baby deer learning to stand for the very first time. A wobbly little Bambi. I'm surprised when she makes it to her knees, even more surprised when she grips the wall and pulls herself up altogether.

I sit back as if settling in. Fold my arms. "What if I can't stand?"

"Get the fuck up, Thomas."

EVA

WHEN IT SEEMS as if one of us might stumble, we each place a hand on the wall, not one another, for support. Halfway through the hallway towards the kitchen, Thomas looks at me. "What now?" he asks.

"Maybe we should say the Mourner's Kaddish."

"Didn't we do that already at the funerals?"

"Maybe we need to say it together."

"And what would that do?"

I can feel a migraine coiling in my right temple. "Hell if I know. Do you have a better idea?"

He opens his mouth, thinks on it, and clamps his lips shut again. I know there is a yahrzeit candle somewhere in this apartment. One I bought but never lit when our mom died. I search the kitchen cabinets for it, slowly as to not inadvertently dislocate something. It takes forever. All the bones in my body feel loose—weakly tethered. Like moving in slow motion.

Finally, I open the door below the sink. That's where I find it—a little glass jar with the prayer label around the front. The wick is still coated in unbroken wax—proof that I've never once lit the thing. I feel bad about that now.

We put the candle on the stove and I find a pack of matches and we light the wick, reciting the half-remembered prayer our mother always had us say on the anniversary of our grandfather's death. The only Hebrew prayer either of us still know with any kind of clarity.

When we're finished, we stand there watching the flame flourish. I close my eyes, because it seems like the appropriate thing to do, but when I open them again, I'm still here. And so is Thomas. It feels anticlimactic.

"What now?"

"Maybe we have to wait until it burns itself out," I suggest.

"How long does that take?"

"A few hours, I think."

He goes and sits down on the couch. There's no more alcohol left in the apartment now. Not for either of us.

DAY SEVEN

EVA

THE YAHRZEIT CANDLE must have gone out in the middle of the night. It's only half burned. And there's a crack down the center of the glass. A little on the nose if you ask me—wrath-of-God type shit—but what do I know? Thomas is still asleep. I don't have it in me to wake him. Not yet. I don't want him to make that offer again. He's too goddamn impulsive.

I fiddle with the Band-Aids on my fingers. I'm afraid if I try to take one off to inspect the damage then the remaining skin will peel with it like chicken grease stuck on tinfoil. My brother stirs, his eyes flitting beneath closed lids. I wonder if he's dreaming—if he's been able to dream since the accident. A part of me, more than just a part if I'm being honest, is envious.

Another fingernail falls off. This time, I don't bother wrapping it. I don't have the energy. Besides, I've grown accustomed to the pain. I wish I was in the bedroom right now with my ceiling cracks. *Four, two, nine.*

THOMAS

SHE'S STARING WHEN I wake up. Like she used to do when I was a baby napping in the crib. At least that's what Mom told us. Evie doesn't remember. Neither do I. In all my memories of Evie, she's distracted—laser focused on whatever little compulsion was sizzling through her brain at any given moment. She never paid me any mind. Not unless it was absolutely necessary. Maybe that's why I was always going out of my way to make it necessary.

We're both still here, which means the candle didn't work. I don't move for fear I will accidentally break a bone or snap my own neck. That's how thin my insides feel. Brittle. Like a fine layer of ice cracking under too much weight. Vision in my bloodshot eye is beginning to go, but I don't tell Evie that. Just like the time I let some hot chick at a party pierce my ear and it got infected but I didn't want to tell anyone. Not Mom. Not Evie. Eventually Evie found out and made me see a doctor about it. A dermatologist. Because even after the infection went away, the skin was still fucked up. She didn't do it because she was worried about me but because it was her friend who had done the piercing in the first place.

"Maybe it's like when you get a piercing but the skin heals wrong," I say then, not looking at her but not looking away either. Just kind of staring into space with my one decent eye. "What if reality healed around the accident in a way that left scar tissue. And now—now reality can't sustain us both."

"Thomas—"

"What if it can't kill one of us so it's killing us both."

"Thomas. Stop it."

"I'll do it," I say. "Really. I don't mind."

I mean it, too. It's my fault anyway—all of it. Maybe not all the shit when we were kids but certainly the shit now. Evie has a life for herself. It looks boring as fuck but it's a life she's living. She never wanted Mom to have me anyway.

Her shoulders straighten. She shakes her head. "No. I'll do it. What the fuck else are big sisters for?"

EVA

THE DAY OF the accident, Thomas showed up on my doorstep. He'd been evicted and needed to borrow some money so that his landlord would let him back in to get some of his shit. I didn't have enough cash and offered to write a check, but Thomas had gotten into trouble forging checks with his landlord before. Fairly, the guy wasn't going to believe my brother unless I was there to sign the paper in front of his own eyes. So, I grabbed my purse and we left.

Thomas drove. We fought the whole way, him bitching about how I was looking down at him for fucking up and me being pissed that I had to spend a goddamn Saturday morning lending money I was never going to get back. He said I shouldn't treat him like such a disappointment and I told him that's what family is: disappointment. There was something he said after that. I don't remember what. And I don't know what I said in return. The truck hit us on the bridge not five minutes from Thomas's apartment. Sent us over the edge. The whole thing might have been easier if we'd both drowned there and then.

SHIVA

I ask Thomas to bring me a knife from the kitchen but when he returns with it in his hand, I can't bring myself to do it. Blood is so slippery. What if I can't do it right? Or don't have the strength? By this point I only have one fingernail left and it's pretty loose. "Let's go to the roof," I say, and that's exactly what we do.

THOMAS

IT'S FREEZING UP here—not windy, just icy in that bone-deep way that stings my throat and my fucked-up eye but seems to numb everything else. Too numbing to even see your breath cloud the air.

"Should we say something first?" I ask her.

She almost laughs. "Like what. A prayer? We already tried that."

"I don't know. Just…something."

"A eulogy?"

I shrug.

Her weight shifts from one foot to the other as she turns in my direction. "What were we talking about?"

"When?"

"Just before we went over the bridge," she says. "Do you remember?" I shake my head and she frowns, disappointment pursed on her lips. Like she thinks I'm lying. "And you really don't want to know how you died?" she asks.

"No. I don't."

EVA

ALL I CAN think about is that xylophone mallet. The swing of it. The blur of color as the little red ball at the end of the wooden stick cut through the air. Poor Thomas's face—filled with such regret. Regret, before he'd even hit me. "That's okay," I tell him. "You don't have to know."

With that, I push Thomas over the edge of my apartment building. It's all one quick motion—easier than it might have been, because he's not expecting it. He doesn't even scream. There's silence, it feels longer than it should, then a thud below as his body hits the ground. You'd assume it would stop traffic or pedestrians, but it doesn't. I don't even look over the side to see if his body is there or if it has vanished with the restoration of whatever timeline we'd damaged.

"I'm sorry," I say, as if an apology and regret are interchangeable. Because I loved him. I did. He was my brother and he was all I had—even when I didn't have him at all—and now I won't ever have him again. It shouldn't surprise me. It shouldn't it shouldn't it shouldn't. But we were always going to end like this. My brother was always going to die. And I was always going to let him. Because I'm a control freak. A coward. Because the ache to return to those cracked ceiling lines is just too goddamn strong. *Four, two, nine.*

Thomas was wrong though. It wasn't his fault. It was mine. I remember now—the last thing I said to him just before the truck hit us. I told him to fuck off and die. And I meant it.

ACKNOWLEDGMENTS

I STILL CAN'T believe this novella found a home—and such a wonderful home, too. *Shiva* is something I worked on in between larger projects, whenever I was feeling dark and dire and needed somewhere to lick my wounds. I loved the challenge of writing oppositional narrating voices—telling the story of two people who cannot help but fall apart together. Sometimes, you just need to write a story that hurts.

There are so many people who supported this book in the journey to publication. I should start with Samantha Carroll, who told me to send the book over after I queried about novella submissions at Dark Matter INK. I'd thank to thank my wonderful editor, Maddy Leary. To Rob Carroll, who saw something in this twisted tale and wanted to publish it—thank you so much. Truly. I am in awe of all you do. Dark Matter INK is the perfect place for *Shiva* and I'm honored to be a part of the catalogue.

I must thank my agent, Jennifer Weltz at the Jean V. Naggar Literary Agency, for being incredible. You believe in my work and champion it so tirelessly. Jennifer, Ariana

Phillips, Cole Hildebrand, and everyone at the Jean V. Naggar Literary Agency—I can never thank you all enough.

Thank you so much to J. A. W. McCarthy and Grace R. Reynolds for reading this early on. I value and trust your opinions beyond measure. Everyone should check out *Sleep Alone* by J. A. W. McCarthy and *Neon Moon* by Grace R. Reynolds. Thank you to Elizabeth Anne Schwartz for your friendship and support. When I first told you about my idea for this novella, you were so excited that it really made me believe this was a story worth pursuing.

Special thanks to my family. This especially goes for my mom, Pauline Verona. You read everything I write. You are there when it's hard and you celebrate every victory with me. I know I've said it before, but I am who I am because of you.

I also need to thank my Anthony. I never could have dreamed of finding such a supportive and caring partner. The universe gave me a gift when it gave me you. Thank you for watching horror movies with me, listening to my ramblings, and telling everyone we meet about my books with such pride and excitement in your eyes.

Last but never least, thank you to my little dog. Phoebe, you don't read but you have spent so many hours watching me write. Essentially, you are co-author to everything I do. I'm so glad we belong to each other. My world is a better place because of it.

—Emily Ruth Verona

ABOUT THE AUTHOR

EMILY RUTH VERONA is the author of *Midnight on Beacon Street*. She received her Bachelor of Arts in Creative Writing and Cinema Studies from the State University of New York at Purchase. She is a Pinch Literary Award winner, a Bram Stoker Awards® nominee, and a Rhysling Award Finalist. Her work has been featured in magazines and anthologies that include *This Way Lies Madness*, *Under Her Skin*, *The Ghastling*, *The Jewish Book of Horror*, *Under Her Eye*, *Monstrous Futures*, *Monster Lairs*, *Strange Horizons*, and *Nightmare Magazine*. She lives in New Jersey with a very small dog.

www.ingramcontent.com/pod-product-compliance
Lightning Source LLC
LaVergne TN
LVHW040105080526
838202LV00045B/3778